W9-AEY-152

Janice Cohn, D.S.W.

Why Did It Happen?

Helping Children Cope in a Violent World

Illustrated by
Gail Owens

Morrow Junior Books New York

This book is dedicated to the scores of young children who spoke with me, drew pictures for me, and even sang to me about the experience of growing up in the often interesting, joyful but sometimes scary world in which we live.

I would like to acknowledge the invaluable help of the following people: Katherine Flynn, David Reuther, and Ellen Dreyer, my editors, for their exceptional skill in helping me to transform thoughts and ideas into words and sentences and, finally, a finished manuscript; Jane Marks, for her insightful critique of the manuscript as well as her encouragement, support and creative ideas; Robin Margent, for her word-processing skills, her uncanny ability to sense when something in the manuscript "just didn't ring true," and her willingness to tell me so; Lynne Smilow, for her encouragement and enthusiasm regarding this project and her wonderful ideas, always generously given; Dr. Jack Clemente, whose special gifts as a child psychiatrist and teacher have enriched this manuscript; Dr. Rona Kurtz, for her sensitive and thoughtful feedback at every stage of this project; and to caring family, friends, and M.M.

Pastels were used for the full-color artwork. The text type is 14-point Goudy Oldstyle.

 Printed in the United States of America. 1 2 3 4 5 6 7 8 9 10

Library of Congress Cataloging-in-Publication Data Cohn, Janice. "Why did it happen?": helping children cope in a violent world / by Janice I. Cohn ; illustrated by Gail Owens. p. cm. Summary: With the help of his parents and teacher, a young boy deals with his feelings about the robbery of the neighborhood grocery store. Includes a note to parents. ISBN 0-688-12312-0 (trade). — ISBN 0-688-12313-9 (library) [1. Violence—Fiction. 2. Crime—Fiction.] I. Owens, Gail, ill. II. Title. PZ7.C665Wh 1994 [E]—dc20 93-1573 CIP AC

NOTE TO PARENTS

Children today live in a violent world. They are bombarded by images of violence in the media and must confront its existence in their society, their local neighborhoods, their schools, and sometimes their own families. When this occurs, children are affected in a number of different ways. For example, when they are repeatedly exposed to acts of violence, their ability to feel safe and secure is seriously undermined. Often, they mimic the violence they see and are more likely to engage in this kind of behavior when feeling angry, frustrated, or overwhelmed.

Television violence also shapes children's perceptions of their world. Though the depiction of such violence is often fictitious, young children, in particular, tend to interpret what they see and hear *literally*. Thus, violence in cartoons or action shows can be just as upsetting to youngsters as the real thing. Additionally, media violence can act as a powerful model for children regarding how to solve problems. If a television or movie hero uses a gun to vanquish the bad guys, how can children be expected to reject the use of violence in their own lives? The fact is, research has shown that the good guys on many television programs actually kill more people than do the villains.

Though children are often upset by violence, they may still take its existence for granted and are not surprised when conflicts are resolved with weapons, fighting, or killing. During the Gulf War, for example, many children were fascinated by images of high-tech weaponry detonating targets in a single flash, but they often did not understand the consequences of warfare—especially the loss of life. Instead, they tended to view the conflict as the ultimate video game, where the opponent best able to "zap" the other became the winner. This does little to foster the concept that fighting should be a last resort in solving problems.

What can parents and teachers do to help counteract the influence of violence upon children?

Parents and teachers can open up a dialogue with children regarding the violence they see and hear around them. For example, while parents cannot always control what their sons and daughters see on television, they can make an effort to watch and discuss selected shows together with their children. Adults can encourage children to think about ways that people (and cartoon characters) can solve problems without hurting and killing one another. They can emphasize that we all have choices regarding how we react to the difficulties that confront us, and that with each choice comes different consequences and responsibilities—a concept that is rarely explored in movies and television shows.

When children are worried about their safety, or the safety of those they love, it helps to emphasize the concrete things that are being done to help protect them. Parents might talk with children about burglar alarms in their homes, police patrols guarding their neighborhoods, and community watch groups that encourage neighbors to look out for one another.

Children should also be reminded of what they themselves can do to increase their own safety, such as remembering their address and phone number and not talking to strangers or wandering off by themselves in public places.

Each child's needs and emotional make-up is different, so it's best for adults to take their cues from the child regarding just how much concrete information he or she needs and wants to hear. What is comforting to one child may provoke discomfort and anxiety in another.

When a violent incident does occur, what helps children cope with their feelings?

Parents and others can help children cope with their emotions by being supportive and loving while *not* minimizing the difficult and painful feelings children may experience. It is important to encourage children to communicate their distress, anger, or anxieties by listening carefully and respectfully to what they have to say and acknowledging their concerns. Not allowing children to talk about a violent event, or trying to distract them, prevents youngsters from using words to express their emotions. When this happens, those emotions are often reflected in nonverbal ways, such as loss of appetite, sleep problems, headaches, stomachaches, and behavior problems.

One way in which young children gain mastery over frightening and upsetting events is by acting them out through play. After experiencing or hearing about a violent event, children may exhibit more violent behavior during playtime. This is perfectly normal and a very positive way of working through some of their feelings of anger and helplessness. However, if a child continually acts out a particular violent event to the exclusion of all other types of play, a mental-health professional should be consulted. Information about acquiring a consultation can be obtained from a community mental-health association, a mental-health clinic, or the pediatric psychiatry department of a hospital or medical center.

Children can often best deal with emotions associated with a violent event when parents discuss specific things that children can do to help make themselves feel better. For example:

When children are feeling anxious and frightened:

- They can talk about their feelings.
- They can discuss with adults the things they can do that will help them be safer.
- They can use their imaginations to create drawings, tell stories, and act out situations similar to real life where *they* choose the endings and *they* choose how the characters react.

When children are feeling sad:

- They can cry if they want to.
- They can reach out to help others who might be feeling sad.
- They can remember happy times they have spent with their family and friends.

When they are feeling angry:

- They can let out their anger in ways that are allowed in the household. For example, they can punch a punching bag as hard as they can.

Whatever the particular feelings children experience, encouraging them to communicate their emotions to the people close to them provides an important outlet. Keep in mind that not every child will want or be able to use words to communicate. Drawing a picture or communicating by a touch or a look can be just as effective if children feel that they are being responded to with warmth and respect.

What can caring adults do to help children develop feelings of compassion and empathy in a violent world?

There are a number of ways that empathy can be fostered in children. These include:

- Setting firm limits and clear guidelines regarding children's actions toward others.
- Making sure children understand that unkind, selfish behavior will not be tolerated, *no matter what the circumstances*.
- Asking children to imagine how *they* would feel if they were the target of mean, hurtful behavior.
- Giving children specific examples of how they can comfort others who are in pain or distress.

Perhaps most important of all is the fact that children learn by *example*. When parents and other role models treat people with compassion and respect, children learn to do the same despite the fact that they live in what is often an unfair, cruel world.

All children will, at some point, be confronted with the existence of violence. There is no way they can be shielded from such knowledge, but opening up a dialogue and sensitively responding to their concerns *does* help. This book is meant to be read to and discussed with children after a violent event has occurred or when children are simply grappling with the implications of living in a violent world.

LOCAL TOMATOES
$3.69
12 PACK

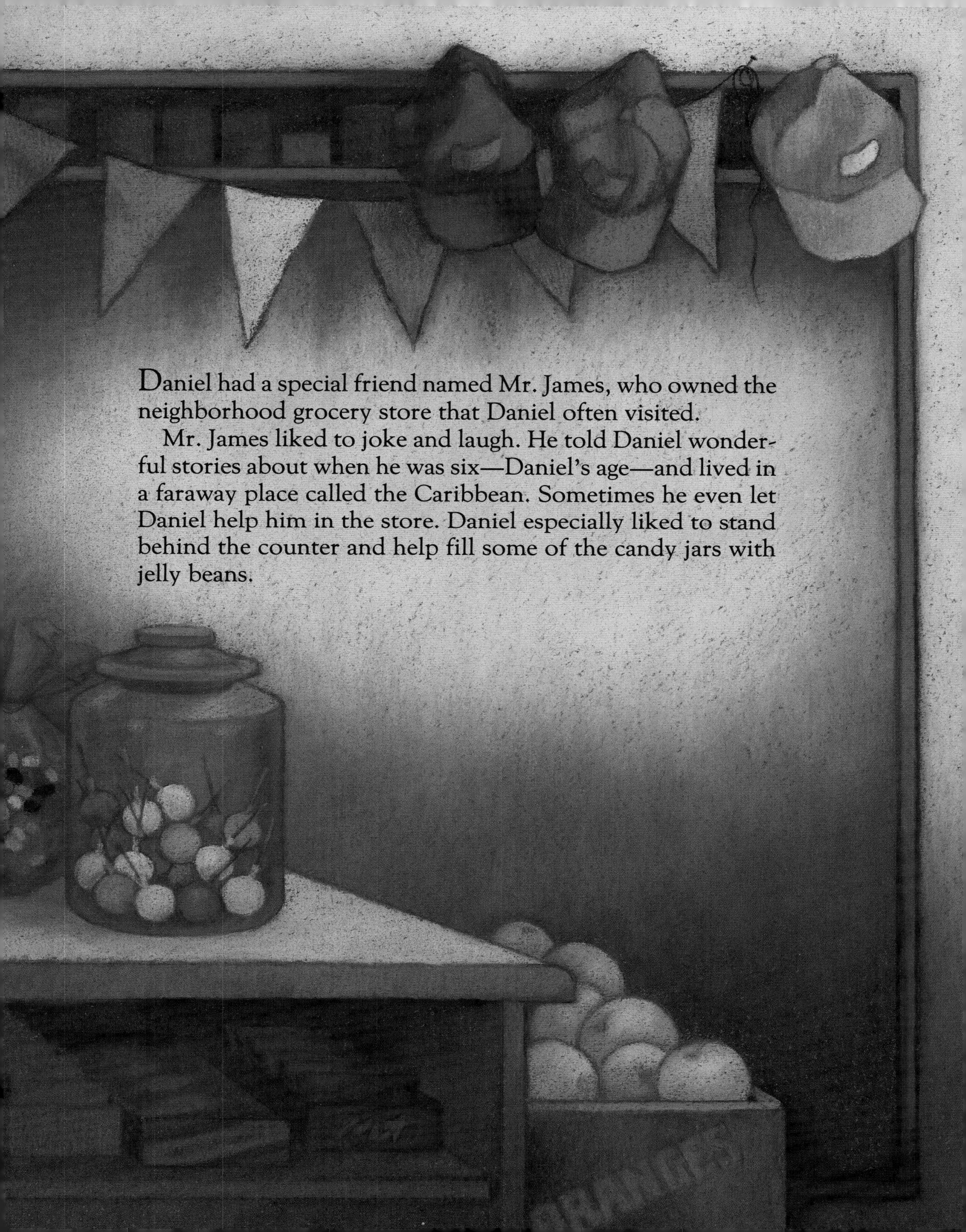

Daniel had a special friend named Mr. James, who owned the neighborhood grocery store that Daniel often visited.

Mr. James liked to joke and laugh. He told Daniel wonderful stories about when he was six—Daniel's age—and lived in a faraway place called the Caribbean. Sometimes he even let Daniel help him in the store. Daniel especially liked to stand behind the counter and help fill some of the candy jars with jelly beans.

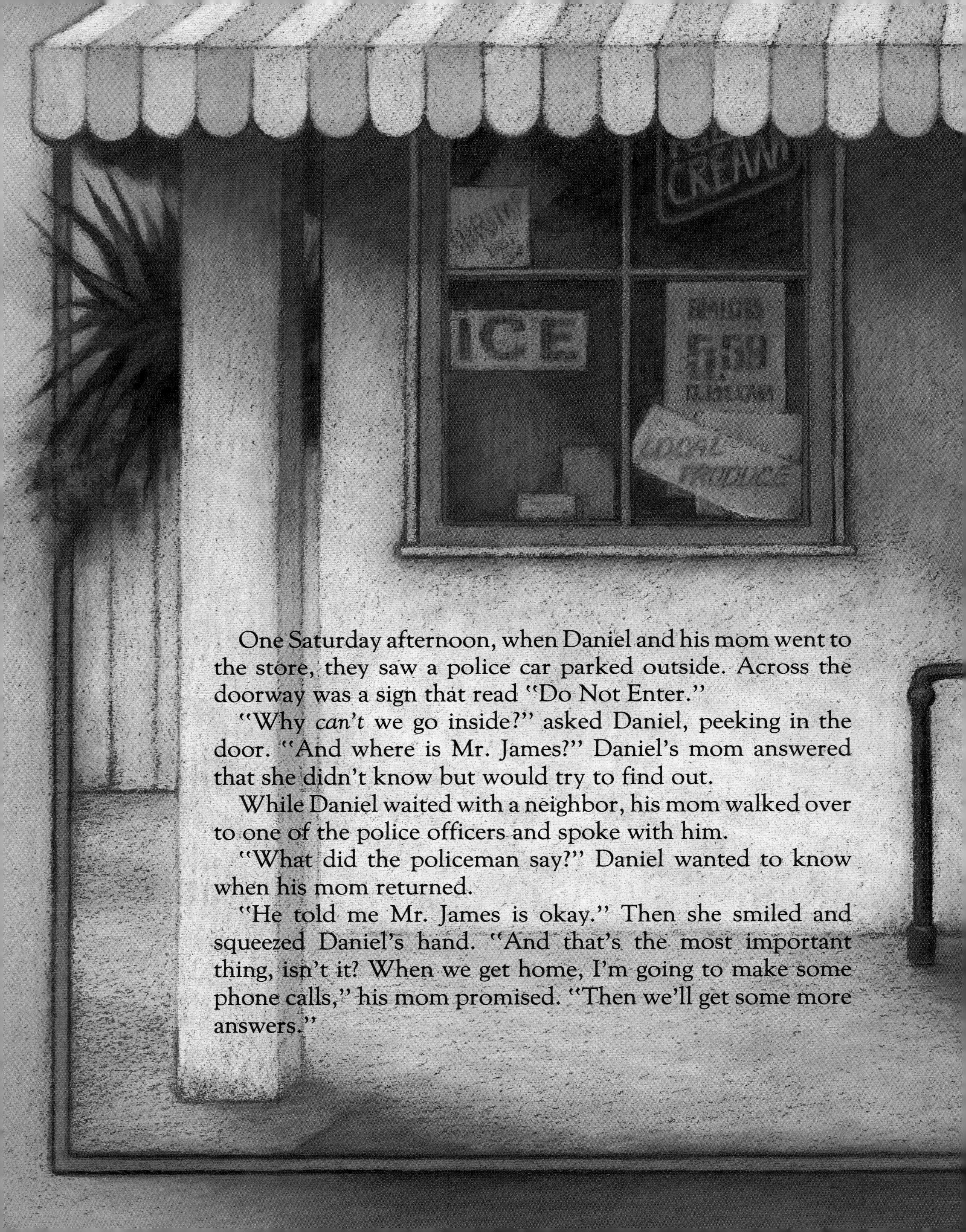

One Saturday afternoon, when Daniel and his mom went to the store, they saw a police car parked outside. Across the doorway was a sign that read "Do Not Enter."

"Why *can't* we go inside?" asked Daniel, peeking in the door. "And where is Mr. James?" Daniel's mom answered that she didn't know but would try to find out.

While Daniel waited with a neighbor, his mom walked over to one of the police officers and spoke with him.

"What did the policeman say?" Daniel wanted to know when his mom returned.

"He told me Mr. James is okay." Then she smiled and squeezed Daniel's hand. "And that's the most important thing, isn't it? When we get home, I'm going to make some phone calls," his mom promised. "Then we'll get some more answers."

53901
DO NO
ENTE

As soon as Daniel and his mom arrived home, Daniel told his dad all about his trip to Mr. James's store. His dad listened very carefully, for he could see Daniel was upset. Then he gave him a hug and said that they would find out what had happened.

A little while later, Daniel's parents came into his room while he was playing with his train set. They sat down next to him and his mom gently told him, "We've found out about Mr. James. Late last night, a man walked into his store and took the money in his cash register."

"That's Mr. James's money!" cried Daniel.

"That's right," his mom replied. "It belongs to Mr. James, not the man who took it."

"But what happened?"

"Mr. James tried to stop him," said his mom. "They struggled and Mr. James's arm was broken. Then the man ran away."

"Is Mr. James okay?"

"Yes, we're sure he is, Daniel," his dad answered. "He went to the doctor, and she put a cast on his arm that will help it heal. Soon it will be as good as new."

Daniel thought for a moment and asked, "Did that man take all Mr. James's money?"

"Yes, honey," said his dad. "We think he did. The police are looking for him right now so that they can arrest him, because what he did was *very* wrong."

"But *why* did he take it? It wasn't his! It was Mr. James's!"

"That's a good question, and a hard one, Daniel," his dad told him. "When people take things that don't belong to them—what we call stealing—they do it for lots of different reasons. Some people have a special kind of problem that makes it hard for them to know right from wrong. Some people were mistreated when they were children, and they grow up with a terrible anger that they take out on others. Sometimes people take drugs or alcohol, and this makes them do things that they would *never* otherwise do. But no matter what reason people have it is always wrong to take something that doesn't belong to them."

Daniel was quiet for a bit as he snuggled up closer to his parents. Then he asked, "Will the police put that man in jail?"

"Yes, when they find him, I think he will go to jail," his dad answered.

"But what if they don't find him?"

"Well, the police are looking hard for clues. That's why Mr. James's store was closed today—so the police could look through it for fingerprints and take pictures."

Daniel thought about this and then he said, "I hope that the robber goes to jail forever and ever and ever!"

"I know how angry you are right now," said Daniel's dad. "Your mom and I feel that way, too. I know one thing we can do to help get out those feelings. Why don't you and I go and hit your punching bag."

"Okay," said Daniel. "I will punch it as hard as I can!"

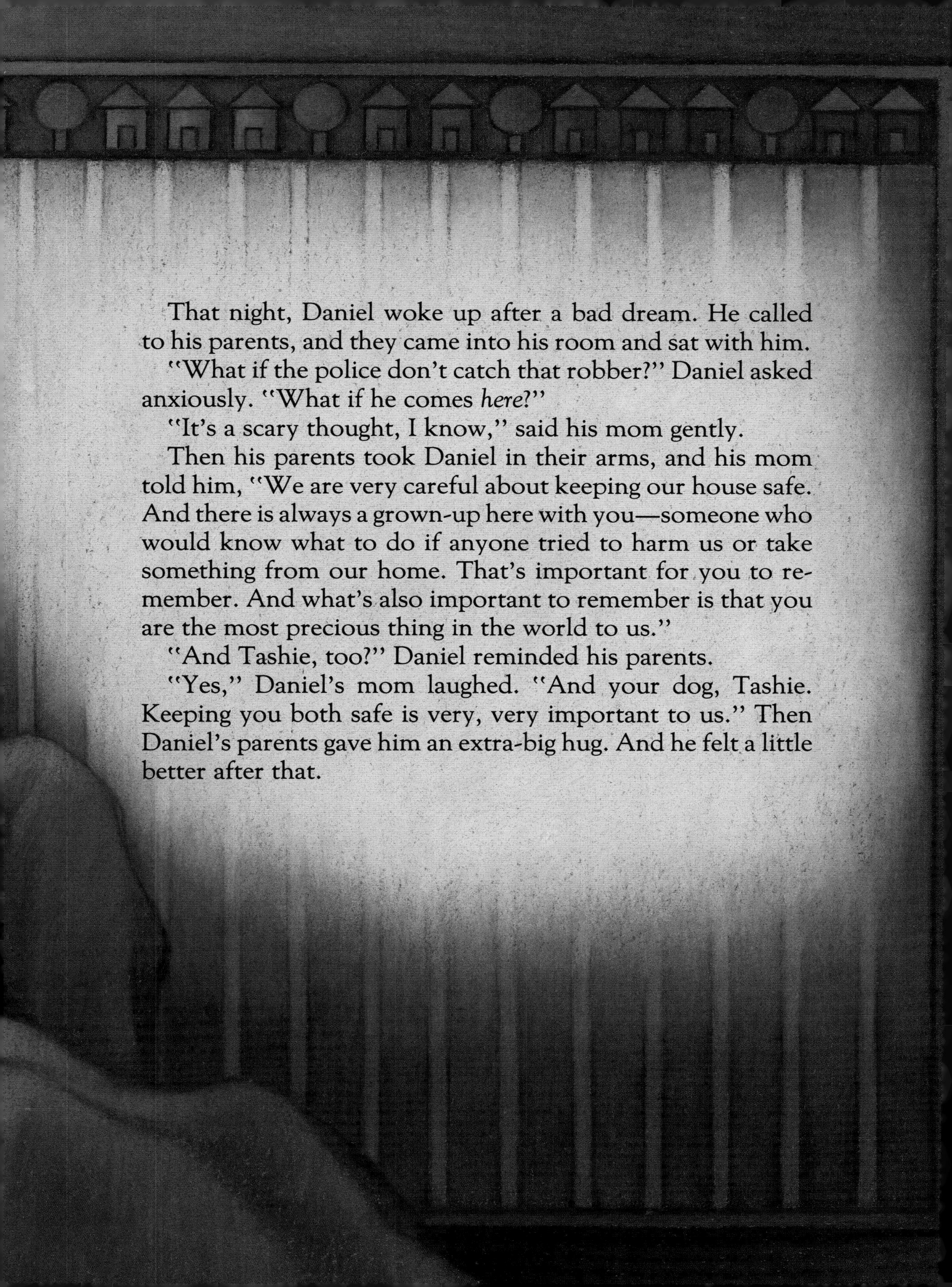

That night, Daniel woke up after a bad dream. He called to his parents, and they came into his room and sat with him.

"What if the police don't catch that robber?" Daniel asked anxiously. "What if he comes *here*?"

"It's a scary thought, I know," said his mom gently.

Then his parents took Daniel in their arms, and his mom told him, "We are very careful about keeping our house safe. And there is always a grown-up here with you—someone who would know what to do if anyone tried to harm us or take something from our home. That's important for you to remember. And what's also important to remember is that you are the most precious thing in the world to us."

"And Tashie, too?" Daniel reminded his parents.

"Yes," Daniel's mom laughed. "And your dog, Tashie. Keeping you both safe is very, very important to us." Then Daniel's parents gave him an extra-big hug. And he felt a little better after that.

Daniel's mom suggested that they go to Mr. James's store to pay him a visit.

"No, I don't want to," Daniel answered. For the store just didn't seem as warm and comforting as it once had been. "But I know what I can do. I can make a special present for Mr. James to make him feel better."

"I think that's a lovely idea," said his mom.

First, Daniel drew lots of hearts on his drawing paper. He knew Mr. James would like that. Then he drew a picture of a man who looked just like what he thought a robber might look like. In Daniel's picture, the man looked as if he were very sorry. And he was giving lots of money to another man—who looked just like Mr. James. Finally Daniel added one more thing, a little boy with a big grin—that was Daniel.

He showed the picture to his mom. She smiled and told Daniel that she was sure Mr. James would like it.

That afternoon, when Daniel's friend Billy came over, Daniel wanted to play a game he called "Chase the Robber." Sometimes Billy was the robber, and sometimes Daniel was. But one thing was always the same: At the end of the game, the two boys had a make-believe gunfight and then the robber was caught.

After a bit, Daniel's parents went over to talk with them.

"We see you two have been doing a lot of shooting at each other," said Daniel's dad.

"Just like I saw on TV," Billy said.

"You're right," agreed Daniel's mom. "There *is* a lot of shooting on some TV shows. But it's usually make-believe, like in your game. We want you boys to understand that in real life, when people shoot each other, they *do* get hurt, and that's a very serious and sad thing. Too many people get hurt that way. What do you boys think you could do in your game to stop the robber without shooting him?"

At first, Daniel and Billy didn't have an answer.

"Think a little harder," Daniel's dad said encouragingly. "This is your game, and you can make anything you want happen if you use your imaginations."

"I know," cried Billy after a few moments. "Maybe someone can use a super karate kick and scare the robber away."

"Or maybe all Mr. James's friends can run after the robber and catch him, and not let him go until the police come," said Daniel.

"Maybe someone can wave a magic wand, and the robber can change into a big kangaroo!" said Billy, who started to giggle.

"That *is* a funny ending," Daniel's dad said, smiling. "In fact, you can make up *lots* of different endings—whatever kinds you want. That's what's so good about make-believe."

On Monday morning, when Daniel went back to school, his teacher asked all the children in the class to sit on their mats for Circle Time. This was a special time each morning when every boy and girl had a chance to talk about anything they wanted to. When it was Daniel's turn, he spoke about what had happened at Mr. James's store. Then the teacher, Mrs. Rose, asked the class to talk about what Daniel had told them.

"I saw a robber on TV once," said Adam.

"Somebody took my bike from me when I was in the park," JoAnn remembered.

"And once someone took my cousin's favorite jacket," Amy said.

"How do you feel when things like that happen?" asked Mrs. Rose.

The children called out lots of different feelings. Sheree said that she got mad. Joshua said that he got scared sometimes. Dawn said that she felt sad—just as if she wanted to cry.

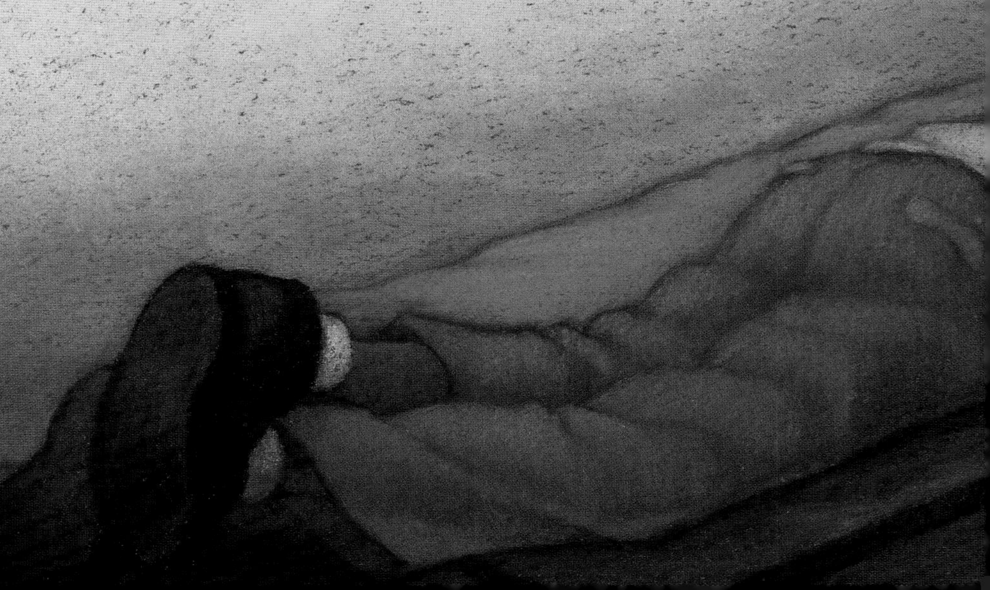

Mrs. Rose nodded after each child spoke. "Yes, those are feelings that *all* of us have sometimes, but we don't all feel the same. When bad or scary things happen, each of us has his or her own special way of feeling. And that's the way it should be.

"So, I have another question for the class. What can we do when we have these feelings to help ourselves feel better? Does anyone have any ideas?"

Daniel raised his hand first and told the class about how he liked to punch his punching bag really hard when he got mad.

Dawn said that when she felt sad, as if she wanted to cry, she *did* cry.

"Does that make you feel better?" asked Mrs. Rose.

"Not every single time," Dawn answered. "Just sometimes."

Jeremy said that when he was feeling scared, he liked to talk with his grandpa. When they were together, he didn't feel afraid anymore.

"When I'm scared, I hug my cat," offered David.

"Yes," said Mrs. Rose. "Those are all good ways that we can comfort ourselves when bad things happen."

After school Daniel's parents came into his room and said they had a surprise for him. Daniel's eyes opened wide and became bright with excitement.

"What is it?" Daniel cried.

"Me," said a familiar voice, and in walked Mr. James. "Your mom told me that you're not quite ready to come back to the store. So I decided to visit you."

Daniel rushed over and they gave each other a big hug. Mr. James showed Daniel his cast and asked him to sign his name on it. There were lots of other names on the cast, as well.

Daniel asked Mr. James if his arm hurt, and Mr. James answered that he was feeling much better. Then they were both quiet for a moment, happy just to be together. But soon, Daniel burst out, "I hope the police catch the man that hurt you and took your money. I wish I could catch him for you, Mr. James!"

"Thank you for wanting to do that for me, Daniel," Mr. James answered warmly. "But you know, the police do that kind of thing very well. And we really have to leave it to them."

Daniel thought for a moment and asked, "Do you think that man might come back to your store?"

"Daniel, I can tell you this: I've done some things to make sure the store is extra safe. I've even put in a special alarm with a button I can press that will ring right in the police station, if I ever need the police."

Daniel was impressed. Then he looked up at Mr. James and asked him, "Are you mad at the man who robbed you?"

"Yes, I'm mad. But I'm not *just* mad. Because even though that man did a very bad thing, there were other people who were very kind and caring to me. Did you know that a man I'd never met before, who was walking past the store when I was hurt, came inside to see if he could help? Then he drove me to the hospital. And when we got to the hospital, the doctor took very good care of me. She's the one who made this cast to help my arm heal.

"After that my friends came to the hospital to take me home and make me comfortable until my son and daughter arrived from out of town. And do you know what else?" Daniel shook his head no. "I've gotten notes and phone calls from a lot of people who shop in the store, letting me know that they care. I even got one very special gift." And Mr. James reached into his pocket and took out Daniel's drawing, which he had carefully folded. That made Daniel smile a big smile.

Then Mr. James told him, "It's true that sometimes bad things happen, even to the people we love and care about. And we may never really understand why. It may make us angry or sad or frightened to think about it. But there *are* things we can do to help people when bad things happen. Just like the help I have gotten. And do you know what else we can do?"

"What?" Daniel asked eagerly.

"We can appreciate the good things that happen—like picnicking in the park, and going sledding in the snow, and just being together with our family and friends who love us. I've especially enjoyed our times together in my store. Would you like to take a walk there now? I can show you all the get-well cards people have sent me, and I sure could use some help filling my jelly bean jars."

"I can help you, Mr. James!" Daniel exclaimed.

"Thank you, Daniel. That means a great deal to me. And so does our friendship."

Later, when he had returned from the store, Daniel thought about what Mr. James had said. He realized that he had helped his friend after all. And it was a very good feeling.